SO-BTZ-630

Luke and Linda each had a toy bank,
a place to save their money.
His looked like a pig, hers like a dog.
Both were cute and funny.

3

When Uncle Mike gave a gift of a crisp paper dollar,
Luke's piggy-bank would smile and light up.
"Oink, oink—thank you—oink," it would holler.

When Aunt Sue gave Linda a quarter, some pennies,
a nickel and dime,
the little doggie-bank jumped up and down,
wagged its tail and barked every time.

They enjoyed helping Mom and Dad do chores,
because earning an allowance is nifty.
"Save it in your banks," the children were told.
"It's a very good thing to be thrifty."

Every time they were given some money they'd say,
"We'll put it here...and thanks!"
Soon the children's coins and paper money bills
started to grow in their banks.

But Luke wanted a new video game controller that cost more than his savings at home. Dad said, "I'll give you the money to pay back later. This is called a loan."

When Luke saved enough to pay back the money,
Dad asked for a little more.
"Money that's loaned earns something called
'interest,' and that's what the extra is for."

When their piggy and doggie banks were full,
Luke and Linda had saved large amounts.
So Dad and Mom took them to the neighborhood
bank where the children opened savings accounts.

Banker Bob and Banker Barb were happy to see
children who know it's smart to save carefully.
Banker Barb said, "One thing to remember
that's kind of simple and funny:
Always save more than you spend
and you'll never run out of money."

"It works like this," said Banker Bob. "Many people join together to give us their money to safely store and use.

Then we loan that money to many more people to pay for special things that they choose."

"They pay the loan back a little at a time,
and some extra interest which is fair and fine.
People who save with us, you and many neighbors,
earn a small part of the interest others pay to enjoy
our bank-loan favors."

"Your savings account money helps our bank make a loan so Jenny's family can buy a new car.

And some of it lets Grandma and Grandpa Roberts take a vacation cruise ship quite far."

"The house for the Garcias is being built with a home-loan from our bank.

And to serve the community with a new restaurant,
Burger World has your savings to thank."

Banker Barb said that when it's college time, families need extra money as a rule.
So there are even special student loans to help kids continue school.

When the bicycle store orders more bikes to sell and puts them on display,
a bank loan lets the store pay later, but you get your new bike today.

When the Widget Company needed a new, bigger factory, owner Jim talked with Banker Bob.

The result was a chance for more good neighbors to find an exciting, well-paying job.

21

Every spring farmer Grady needs extra money to buy seeds to plant on his land.

Then in fall he has corn and pumpkins to sell thanks to his bank's helping hand.

Bank people, called "tellers," keep track of our money with computers and high-tech machines. When we're away on a trip we use an ATM for banking. "Automatic teller" is what that means.

It's faster and easier for banking sometimes if Mom and Dad use the drive-thru teller lines.

There are banks in big cities in buildings quite tall.
And there are little banks in tiny buildings in
suburbs and towns quite small.

BANK CENTER

PiZ
PLAC

Banks help moms and dads pay all the bills,
right down to the food we eat.
Using bank checks and debit cards
for money can't be beat.

27

Banks follow rules to keep money safe and ready. Even the President and a special government department are there to keep things steady.

TREASURY DEPARTMENT

So, the idea that starts with Linda's doggie bank
and Luke's happy little pig
is really the same way banks help us save--
the only difference, they're big.

Think just how much banks do for us so we can enjoy every day.